THE WHITE ROOM

ROOM

JANICE GREENE

SADDLEBACK
EDUCATIONAL PUBLISHING

❚Q❘READS

SERIES 1

Black Widow Beauty
Danger on Ice
Empty Eyes
The Experiment
The Kula'i Street Knights
The Mystery Quilt
No Way to Run
The Ritual
The 75-Cent Son
The Very Bad Dream

SERIES 2

The Accuser
Ben Cody's Treasure
Blackout
The Eye of the Hurricane
The House on the Hill
Look to the Light
Ring of Fear
The Tiger Lily Code
Tug-of-War
The White Room

SERIES 3

The Bad Luck Play
Breaking Point
Death Grip
Fat Boy
No Exit
No Place Like Home
The Plot
Something Dreadful Down Below
Sounds of Terror
The Woman Who Loved a Ghost

SERIES 4

The Barge Ghost
Beasts
Blood and Basketball
Bus 99
The Dark Lady
Dimes to Dollars
Read My Lips
Ruby's Terrible Secret
Student Bodies
Tough Girl

SADDLEBACK
EDUCATIONAL PUBLISHING
www.sdlback.com

ISBN-13: 978-1-61651-197-5
ISBN-10: 1-61651-197-4
eBook: 978-1-60291-919-8

Printed in the U.S.A.

19 18 17 16 15   3 4 5 6 7

■ ■ ■

When Andy rang the doorbell, the door opened immediately. "Marcus Chiang?" Andy asked.

The man in the doorway looked him up and down. He had a square face and thick eyebrows. His mouth was a thin line drawn across his face. He gave Andy the slightest of nods and opened the door a little wider.

Andy lifted his toolbox and stepped inside. "Andy Yeung," he said, smiling and sticking out his hand.

Marcus ignored the hand. "This way," he said, walking down a wide hallway.

Andy raised an eyebrow and followed Marcus through the apartment. The rooms were large, empty, and silent. There were tables and chairs of polished, dark wood, tall vases on pedestals, and elaborate paintings wider than his arms could stretch. Andy felt like he was in a museum.

"Big place you've got here, Marcus," Andy remarked.

Marcus turned to face him. "Call me Mr. Chiang," he said coldly.

Andy thought of something else he'd like to call him, but kept his mouth shut. He needed the money.

The bedroom had a king-sized bed and two big bay windows.

"Here," said Marcus, stopping in front of the windows.

Frowning, Andy bent over to take a closer look. The wood was gray and cracked from water damage. He pushed his thumbnail into a windowsill. The texture of the wood was like a sponge.

"You've got a lot of water damage here. I'd have to take out both windows and replace them," Andy said.

He expected Marcus to ask how much it would cost, but he didn't. "How long will that take?" he said.

Andy said, "Two weeks—unless you want me to get another guy in to help."

"No," Marcus said shortly.

"At least it's spring," Andy said. "So you won't have a lot of stormy weather blowing in. And I'll be careful not to inconvenience your family too much—"

"I live alone," said Marcus.

"Oh, I just assumed—" Andy said, glancing at the wide bed.

"My wife died two years ago," said Marcus.

"I'm sorry," Andy said, noticing that Marcus didn't look very sorry.

"Do you listen to the radio while you work?" Marcus asked.

"Sometimes—if there's a ballgame on," Andy replied.

"You can listen to the radio. I'll bring one in," said Marcus.

"Okay," Andy said. Something in Marcus's face told him not to ask why.

■ ■ ■

Most important thing," Marcus said, "—you stay in *this room*. No other rooms! You eat lunch here and don't leave until I get home." He stared hard at Andy, as if expecting him to protest.

Andy's neck burned, but he nodded. It was clear he'd lose the job if he didn't go along with Marcus's rules.

When Andy arrived the next morning, Marcus had already set up a radio and turned it up loud. Andy switched it off as soon as the man left for work. Then he strolled around the apartment, poking into every room. He'd never done this on a job—but until now, no one ordered him to stay in one room.

There was the kitchen, large and spotless, and the formal dining room, with six chairs lined up as straight as soldiers at the gleaming dark table. The living room had stiff-looking chairs and a couch. The bed in the bedroom was as neatly made as one in a hotel room. There were no magazines, no clothes draped over chairs, and no stray mugs or plates around the TV. It wasn't at all like Andy's apartment.

The door next to the bedroom was locked. Andy jiggled the door handle, shrugged, and started to work.

He took a crowbar and started prying the rotten wood away from the wall. The window was redwood. It had once been beautiful. He wondered why Marcus, with his magazine-perfect apartment, had let his windows become ruined.

Around noon, he stopped and ate a sandwich. It was so quiet he could hear himself chew. Eight stories below, the city traffic was a quiet hum. Twice he heard the distant slam of a door in another apartment. That was all.

He went back to work, carefully lifting glass from the rotted sashes, when suddenly the back of his neck prickled. He turned around quickly, scanning the empty room. He'd been sure that someone was watching him!

A while later, Andy again got the feeling that he was being watched. He spun around in time to see the "locked" door move from slightly open to closed. He walked over and tapped on it.

"Who's there?" he asked loudly. "What's going on?"

He stopped and listened—but the dead silence of the apartment fell around him like a blanket. Now he wondered if he'd been imagining things. He shook his head and went back to the windows. Finding a rock station on the radio, he turned it up loud. The place was just *too* quiet.

At 5:30 sharp, Marcus Chiang came home and inspected Andy's work. He brushed a piece of lint off his expensive suit and gave a slight nod. Andy got the impression that the work he'd done wasn't great—but it would have to do. Andy had intended to ask him about the locked room. But as he looked at Marcus's tight face, he changed his mind. He left, happy to get back to the noise and color of the bustling streets.

■ ■ ■

Andy had no time to go home. He bought a sandwich, which he ate while waiting for the streetcar out to City College. That night he had a quiz in anatomy and an endless lab session in physiology to look forward to.

It was almost 10:00 when he got to his basement apartment. It smelled heavily of pizza. His roommate, Wes, had taken over the living room. He and three of his friends were playing video games. Andy closed the door to his room, stuffed cotton in his ears, and studied until 1:00 in the morning.

The next morning, he overslept. "Seven minutes late," Marcus scolded with an accusing glare.

"Sorry," Andy muttered, seeing that *no* excuse would be accepted.

When Marcus left, Andy quickly set to work. He wanted this job finished.

"Seven minutes late," he muttered between his teeth. Then he carelessly jerked a pane of glass from the sash bar. When it shattered, his hand was lined with red streaks. *"Auuuugh!"* he yelled, doubling over in pain.

■ ■ ■

Soft footsteps pattered up behind him. He caught a glimpse of a young woman's face. But then she bent over his hand and her black hair hid her face.

She wrapped his hand in a towel and pressed it against his stomach. The strength of her fingers surprised him. "Hold it still," she said. Then she ran to the bathroom, her bare feet almost soundless on the floor.

In a flash she returned with a first-aid kit. Once more she bent over the hand, swabbing the cuts with antiseptic. He looked away, feeling sick and weak.

"The little finger's been hurt the worst," she murmured. "You're probably going to need some stitches."

A few minutes later, his hand was clean and bandaged. Except for his little finger, the pain wasn't so bad now.

"Hey, thanks a lot!" he said, but the young woman wasn't listening. She was staring at her white pants. A red dot of blood had stained the material.

Then she grabbed the first-aid kit and snatched up the bloody cotton swabs from the floor. "Excuse me, please. I have to take care of this!" she said, gesturing at the bloodstain.

"Wait a minute!" Andy cried, moving toward her.

"No! You should leave now! You need stitches in your finger!" she said. Her eyes were wide with panic as she ran across the bedroom. Andy caught a glimpse of white as she hurried through the door. Then he heard the click of a lock.

Andy took the streetcar to the city clinic. After waiting an hour and a half, a tired intern saw him and put three stitches in his little finger. After that, Andy went home and studied for an anatomy test. Every once in a while he closed his eyes, trying to remember the young woman's pretty face.

■ ■ ■

The minute Marcus left the apartment the next morning, Andy knocked on the locked door. From inside the room, a sweet female voice said, "Is your hand all right?"

"Can I come in?" said Andy. "Or can you come out here?"

The door opened and the young woman stepped out, closing the door behind her. She was the same height as Andy, with a round face and pale skin. Today she wore her hair in a thick, glossy braid that fell below her shoulders. Some might not call her beautiful, he thought, but to him she was absolutely stunning.

"I'm Andy Yeung," he said.

"My name is Lily Chiang," she said.

"You're Marcus's—" he began.

"Wife," she said.

Andy was confused. "Why are you staying in that room all day?" he asked. "What are you doing in there?"

"Oh, I like it there," she said.

"I don't get it. Does he *make* you stay in there?" Andy said.

Lily's hands fluttered nervously. She asked, "How is your hand?"

"It's okay—thanks to *you,* Lily. I'm really very grateful. Tell me—don't you ever go out?" Andy asked.

"Outside?" she said.

"Yeah, *outside,*" said Andy.

She looked away. Andy saw that her hands were shaking. "Oh, no, I can't," she said nervously.

"You're kidding me! When was the last time you stepped out of this apartment?" Andy said.

■ ■ ■

In one quick movement, she stepped back into the room and locked the door.

Andy stood for a moment, staring at

the door. Then he shrugged and returned to work. He kept the radio off, his ears straining for sounds behind the door. But he heard nothing all the long day.

The next morning, Andy knocked softly on the door. "Lily? May I come in? May I see your room?" he asked. His voice was gentle.

The door opened slowly. As Andy stepped forward, he felt like he was inside a cloud. Everywhere—hung by threads from the ceiling—there were delicate objects made of white paper. He looked closer and saw that they were paper birds, hundreds of them!

Lily smiled shyly. "I make a new one every day," she said.

Every day. Andy thought of prisoners marking time on cell walls and felt a chill at her words. He looked around the room. The walls and ceiling were white. Even the *floor* was white! The place was as clean as a new sheet of paper. There were two shelves full of books, a TV, a desk, a small couch, and a set of barbells neatly laid out on the floor.

"You lift weights?" he asked.

"Oh, yes, every day," she said with a light little laugh. "Marcus doesn't want me to get fat."

Marcus. "So that's *it?* You read, watch TV, and lift weights—what else do you do?" Andy asked.

Lily thought for a moment. "I clean the apartment—and when Marcus comes home, I cook dinner," she said.

"Would you like to have lunch with me?" Andy asked.

"Yes, thank you," Lily said, looking directly into his eyes for the first time. The warmth of her eyes made Andy feel light, as if he was suspended in air like one of her white birds.

Sitting cross-legged behind him, she watched him work. The April sun came through the window, throwing soft shadows on the floor. Andy told her about his classes, and his goal of becoming a physical therapist. She told him about a movie she'd seen on TV.

Luckily, he'd brought an extra peanut

butter sandwich. "This is good," she said. "Marcus usually likes lamb chops."

Marcus. Even the man's name made Andy grit his teeth. "Are you in love with him?" he said.

"Well, he's my *husband,*" said Lily. She looked out the window. "He takes care of me," she added.

"Then why can't you go outside?" Andy demanded. "Is that what he calls taking care of you—keeping you cooped up in here all day?"

"I like it here," said Lily.

"That's not a life, staying home all day! That's stupid!" said Andy.

Lily stood up quickly. "Don't knock on the door again," she said. Then she hurried back to her room.

■ ■ ■

Andy left the apartment, sticking a folded piece of paper in the front door to keep it from locking. He took the streetcar home and was back in an hour, carrying a plastic crate. In front of Lily's door, he opened the crate and a large, rough-faced, orange cat walked out. The big cat paced in front of the door and meowed loudly.

"Pumpkin hates closed doors," Andy announced. "You can't even close the door if you're taking a bath."

Lily opened the door. "Oh!" she said, smiling with delight as Pumpkin rubbed against her legs.

"I knew I guessed it right! You *are* a cat person," said Andy delightedly.

"Yes, I am!" said Lily. "And you're such a beautiful cat!" she crooned as she bent down to scratch Pumpkin's chin. Andy was surprised to see that Lily was crying. She quickly wiped the tears away and smiled up at him.

"Lily, let's go outside!" Andy said.

She stared at him, wide-eyed.

"Come on! The weather is great! The park will be beautiful," said Andy.

Lily hesitated. She looked down. "I can't," she finally said.

"Why not?" Andy asked gently.

She stared at the floor. "I'm insane," she said in a soft whisper.

"What?" Andy cried. "What do you mean? Insane how?"

"I'm not rational," she said. "I can't cope with real life."

"Oh, come on!" Andy scoffed. "I don't believe that for a minute."

"It's true," Lily said sadly. "Marcus takes care of me so I don't have to stay in a hospital."

Marcus. "Did you see a doctor? Have you been diagnosed?" said Andy.

"No—but I know it's true," she said.

"Look, it won't hurt you to come to the park," Andy insisted. "I'll be there with you. It'll be all right."

She shook her head and turned away.

■ ■ ■

Andy took Pumpkin back home, and then returned to the Chiangs' apartment. By now, one of the windows had been completely removed. Andy had covered the empty frame with heavy blue plastic. Lily came out to see him in the afternoon. While she watched him work, he tried to convince her that a trip to the park would be fun and easy. Then, just before Marcus came home, she finally agreed.

The next morning, when Andy woke up, he hurried to the high window in his bedroom. Seeing a clear sky, he sighed with relief.

Marcus left even quicker than usual that day. He didn't even quiz Andy about the work he'd be doing. As Andy heard the door lock behind him, excitement rose in his chest. He bent to rearrange the wood and nails, making it look like he'd been working. Then something caught his eye. It was a tiny, white bowl, the kind you'd fill with a spoonful of jam or dipping sauce. There were several orange cat hairs in it! Andy wondered if Lily had put them there. He decided to ask her later, but then her door opened. The sight of her sweet face made him forget everything.

She had on a red warm-up jacket that looked like it had never been worn before. Her hands twisted nervously.

"Let's go!" he said.

She followed him out the door and into the hallway. They went down in the elevator, out the entrance, and down the front steps. On the bottom step they paused, taking in the bright spring day.

The sidewalk was crowded with hurrying people. Two motorcycles roared past. A toddler wailed loudly, and a big delivery truck made shrill beeps as it backed into a parking space.

Lily froze, her mouth tight with apprehension. Andy took her hand and pulled her gently forward. She pulled back, almost making him trip.

"Hey, you're *strong!*" Andy said, laughing. "When we come back, you can help me pry some of that wood loose."

Her face relaxed, and she smiled.

"The park is full of birds," he said, hoping it was true.

They stepped into the stream of foot traffic. Lily almost walked into a man carrying two bags of groceries.

"Watch it!" the man said sharply. Lily shrank back as if she'd been hit. Andy held her hand as they walked on.

■ ■ ■

The park *was* full of birds that day. There were sparrows, pigeons, and a noisy flock of blackbirds on the grass. Then Andy remembered the lake. He showed Lily the way. It was crowded with ducks, and there was also a lovely white bird with a finger-thin neck and very long legs.

"It's an egret," Lily told him. "I saw one just like it on TV."

The blooming plum trees looked like enormous, pink cushions. Andy and Lily walked under clusters of blossoms still wet with dew. He held down a branch so she could smell the sweet scent of the blossoms.

Lily moved her face from side to side, letting the petals brush against her cheeks.

"Look, you've got some in your hair!" Andy laughed. He reached to brush the petals away—and then she was in his arms and they were kissing!

"You're not crazy, Lily," he whispered, burying his face in her hair. "You're *not.*" He held her, wanting never to let go.

They didn't think about the time until Andy's stomach started growling. He looked at his watch and was surprised to see that it was already two o'clock.

"Why don't we get something to eat and then head back?" he said.

"Oh, no!" Lily cried, a worried look crossing her face. "We must go back right away. I can make something to eat at the apartment."

To save time, they took the express bus. When it arrived at the stop, Lily put her fingers in her ears at the sound of the screeching brakes. She walked up the steps, past the bus driver.

"Fare!" barked the driver, a heavy-set man with a bristly blond mustache.

Lily turned to Andy in confusion. "I—uh—don't have any money," she said.

Andy paid their fares, wondering if his slim supply of money would last until Marcus paid him.

Lily kept looking at Andy's watch. She sighed with relief when they reached the apartment building at 2:45. In the elevator, she noticed a grass stain on the knee of her pants.

■ ■ ■

You're worried about Marcus," Andy said with a trace of sarcasm.

She looked at him. "It's not a good idea to make Marcus angry," she said.

"I'm sorry about that. What did you do with those other pants—the ones with the bloodstain?" he said.

"I hid them," Lily said in a hushed voice as she unlocked the door and stepped into the apartment.

Andy grabbed her hands. "Does he hurt you, Lily?"

She turned her face away.

"Does he?" Andy insisted.

"A little," she said.

"A *little?* What does that mean? What does he do? I care about you, Lily!" Andy cried. Then he noticed that her eyes were shut tight, and he gathered her close. "Tell me," he said softly.

"He hits me sometimes, and—he killed my cat. He threw her from the window." She was crying now.

"Oh, Lily," Andy said sympathetically.

"When we were married," she began to explain, "I was unhappy almost right away. I told him I wanted to leave. He started waking me up at night, telling me I was irrational. I could never sleep. Sometimes he hid all the food for days. I was afraid I would starve. I *felt* insane. I don't know—maybe I was."

"He's an evil man, Lily. Let's leave—now!" said Andy. "You can stay with me."

Her eyes were terrified. "I can't! I've been with Marcus for more than two years now, Andy. I don't know how to do anything!" she said.

"You can! I'll help you," Andy begged. "Don't you want to be with me?"

The look on her face made his heart turn to water. "I want to be with you every minute," she said.

They agreed that Lily would leave Marcus tomorrow. Andy would come at his regular time, help her pack a few things, and they'd go.

Andy didn't dare look at Marcus when he came home from work. He was afraid his face would give him away. Luckily, Marcus dismissed him quickly.

■ ■ ■

On the way home, Andy's mind swirled with images of Lily. When he reached his apartment, a notice from the landlord greeted him. Rent was going up by 15 percent—effective immediately!

Reality hit him like a splash of cold water. What was he doing, begging Lily to come live with him? He was just a student who could barely pay the rent! He remembered Lily's reluctance to leave her apartment, and her awkwardness on the bus. How could she ever hold a job? She was as helpless as a small child.

That night, after he returned from class, he lay in bed, unable to sleep. He loved Lily—or thought he did. But he kept imagining what it would be like if they were together. He'd be off at work or school and she'd be sitting around the apartment all day, playing with Pumpkin and watching TV. *You'll be sick of her in six months,* he told himself.

The sky had turned from black to gray when he finally drifted off to sleep. When he woke, he felt tired, but full of cold resolve. He would get Lily away from Marcus Chiang—but then he'd have to let her go. She must have family somewhere. Or maybe she could go to a women's shelter.

He had barely enough money to live on. The last thing he needed was a helpless woman hanging around his neck.

■ ■ ■

When Marcus answered the door that morning, Andy thought there was something strange about him. But he wasn't sure what it could be.

Andy walked down the silent hallway as he did every morning, with Marcus following right behind him. Suddenly Andy realized what had seemed odd: Marcus was holding one arm stiffly at his side. His hand was cupped—as if he was hiding something!

Andy wondered what was going on. He glanced back at Marcus and saw a flash of steel!

Andy cried out in pain and anger as a long knife ripped into his shoulder. When Marcus raised the knife again, Andy kicked him in the shin and sprinted to the window. As he passed the white room, he looked inside and caught a glimpse of Lily. Her upper body was tied to a dining room chair! Her head drooped on her chest.

Andy looked about frantically for something to use as a weapon. His tools were gone! Then Marcus was on him again, thrusting wildly with the knife. Andy grabbed Marcus's wrist, making him squeal in pain. Then, from the corner of his eye, Andy saw Lily. The chair was on her back as she crab-walked silently toward them on bare feet. What courage! But Andy wondered what she could possibly do to help.

■ ■ ■

Step by step, Marcus was forcing him back toward the window. Andy struggled, but the searing pain in his shoulder weakened him. Andy's fist caught Marcus on the chin. But then Marcus grabbed his arm and pushed him backward. Andy felt the window ledge against the back of his legs. The breeze was rustling through the plastic. "I'm throwing you out—like trash!" Marcus thundered. Andy desperately grabbed at the man's neck, but Marcus reared back and gave him a mighty kick in the stomach.

Andy toppled over the window ledge. For a moment, the plastic held him, but then it tore away. Desperately, Andy lunged and caught hold of the window ledge! He dangled helplessly, the ragged plastic flapping against his legs. He looked up to see Marcus's face twisted in an ugly grin. The crazed-looking man started to raise his knife hand.

Then Andy saw Lily coming up behind Marcus. She swung the legs of the chair, whacking his legs and nearly sending him over the ledge. *"Arrrugh!"* Marcus yelled. He grabbed the ledge and tried to right himself. But he had lost his balance. Again, Lily slammed the chair legs against her husband's side. At that, Marcus gasped, swayed, and then toppled into the empty air! As the man fell, Andy caught a glimpse of his face, frozen with surprise and horror.

Lily backed up, moving the chair so it hung on the ledge. The legs were within Andy's reach! Lily twisted her head around to see him. Groaning with effort, Andy reached out and grasped a leg. The pain in his shoulder was awful.

"Andy! Grab on with both hands!" Lily ordered.

Andy tried to reach, but spots were gathering before his eyes.

Lily sensed his weakness. *"Hurry!"* she cried fiercely.

His hand closed around a rung of the chair. "Hold on!" she yelled. Slowly, with great effort, she dragged him up, up. His arms were past the ledge now. Then he finally felt his ribs scraping over the top of the ledge. He let go and collapsed to the floor. For a second, the spots before his eyes grew larger. Then there was nothing but darkness.

When Andy came to, he saw Lily bent over the phone. Still tied to the chair, she was holding a pencil in her teeth, punching in numbers. In spite of his pain, Andy smiled. He knew he'd never find another woman as brave or strong or beautiful as Lily Chiang.

■ ■ ■

After Marcus died, Lily never went into the white room again. She sold the apartment right away and bought a small condo downtown. First, she got a job as a clerk. Then later, she trained to become a counselor at a women's shelter. At night, she started taking some courses in physical education at City College.

It was a year and a half later when Andy finally earned his degree. He was immediately offered a job at General Hospital. That was when he asked Lily to marry him—and she said yes.

After-Reading Wrap-Up

1. Who do you think left the cat hairs in the dish?

2. Why did Marcus let his windows get ruined?

3. What activity did Lily do in the white room that saved Andy's life—and perhaps her own?

4. Marcus seldom appears and has very little to say in the story. Is it easy to forget about him? Why or why not?

5. *The White Room* had some action and some romance. Which did you prefer? Explain your answer.

6. In the end, Lily was able to cope with the world outside. Did this seem believable to you? Why or why not?